For everyone who's told me they can't draw!
– Heath McKenzie

Little Hare Books
an imprint of
Hardie Grant Egmont
Ground Floor, Building 1, 658 Church Street
Richmond, Victoria 3121, Australia

www.littleharebooks.com

Copyright © Heath McKenzie 2019

First published 2019

 A catalogue record for this
book is available from the
National Library of Australia

978 1 760680 18 3 (hbk)

Designed by Hannah Janzen
Produced by Pica Digital, Singapore
Printed through Asia Pacific Offset
Printed in Shenzhen, Guangdong Province, China

5 4 3 2 1

Archie
the Arty Sloth

HEATH McKENZIE

LITTLE  HARE
www.littleharebooks.com

Archie was **bored**.

This happened surprisingly often, given that Archie was a sloth.

Most sloths liked
to slump and doze
and sloth around.

But Archie was an
unusually active sloth!

The other sloths did
their best to keep
Archie occupied.

But they could only find so many tangled things to untangle, or containers to match with lids, or Sudokus to Sudoku.

Then one day, a sloth returned from a six-month journey to the ground and back. The sloth brought exotic gifts and trinkets – and most importantly, it brought back something for Archie.

"Masterpiece Mandrill's 1000-piece Art Set!"

Archie marvelled as the other sloths heaved sighs of relief.

At first, Archie dabbled in
a few different things.

He tried **this**.

And he tried **that**.

And he even tried
THAT!

But finally Archie
decided where his artist's
heart truly lay ...

He was a PAINTER!

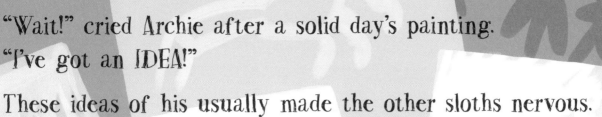

"Wait!" cried Archie after a solid day's painting. "I've got an IDEA!"

These ideas of his usually made the other sloths nervous.

"We should put on an art show," Archie declared. "There's plenty of paint here for EVERYONE!"

Archie made it as easy as possible for everyone to join in.

Amazingly, the other sloths were quite happy to be involved. In fact, the results were quite impressive ... eventually.

Archie eagerly inspected everyone's paintings.

First he admired them ...

then he just
looked at them ...

and **eventually** he preferred to sort of squint at them.

Soon the jungle was transformed into a high class, top end art gallery, full of bold and daring works.

And then there's mine, thought Archie glumly.

Archie sighed. "Mine is all wrong. I can't do art."

He decided it would be best to take his painting home ...
but there was no time! Art lovers were arriving, so Archie
quickly hid behind his painting instead.

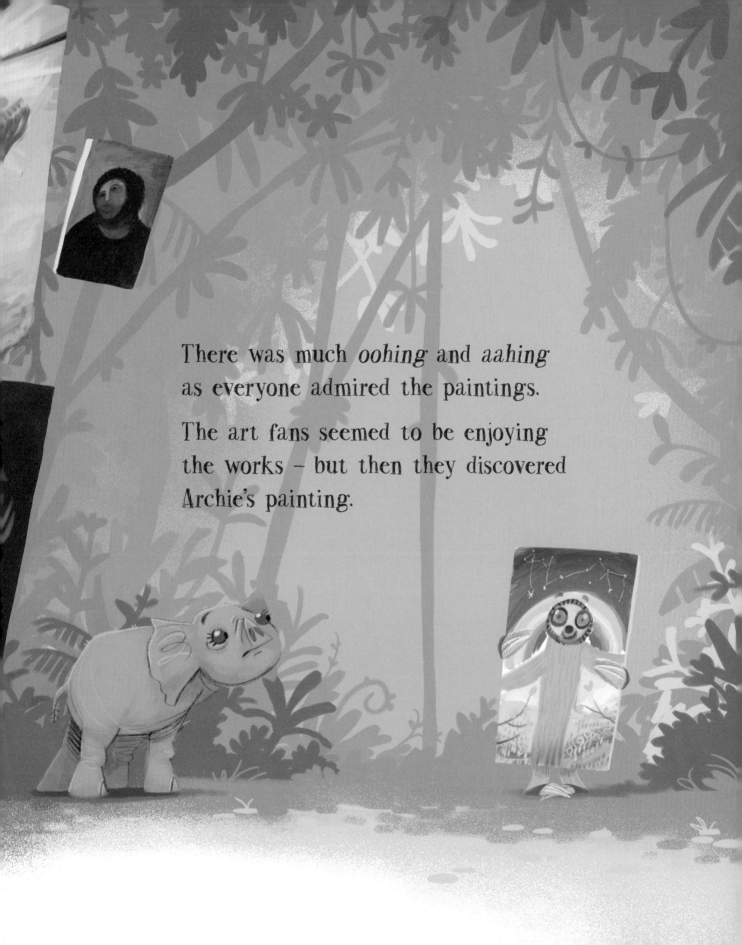

There was much *oohing* and *aahing*
as everyone admired the paintings.

The art fans seemed to be enjoying
the works – but then they discovered
Archie's painting.

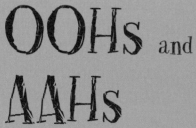

OOHs and AAHs
were replaced with
WOWs and
AMAZINGs!

Archie was

baffled.

He stepped out from behind his work.

"I don't understand," he said. "I can't really draw hands, or faces … or bodies or eyes or noses. I'm no good at feet …

and I definitely can't do mouths. I'm not a proper painter. Not like the other sloths."

"Maybe not," came a voice from the crowd.
"But you can do THIS!"

Archie gasped –
it was Masterpiece
Mandrill himself, and
he was pointing right
at Archie's painting!

"That's the beauty of art," Mandrill continued. "There is no right or wrong way to do it! It doesn't matter that your art doesn't look like everyone else's –

how you paint is how YOU paint!"

And so from that day on
Archie did exactly that –

he painted how HE painted!